The Moon Orchid
Who Loved
The Prince
That Limped

By

Mark A. Sather

The Moon Orchid Who Loved
The Prince That Limped
By
Mark A. Sather

Copyright © 2015 by Mark A. Sather

Cover illustration by Mark A. Sather

Table of Contents

1. The Moon Orchids

When the earth was young, but a child as worlds go, moon orchids were everywhere. They covered entire valleys like a sea of glowing light, with its waves dancing in the night wind. The moon shone brighter in those days. That was because the moon goddess, Seralyn, was filled with love for her children, the moon orchids. The more love she felt, the brighter she shined.

When men and women first came into the world, they too loved the moon orchids. They knew they were the children of the moon goddess; therefore humans honored the moon orchids. Children would beg their parents to take them on a moonlight walk to see the orchids. "Mother! Father!" the children would cry, "Please, take us to see the moon orchids." Their parents would smile, as they remembered when they were their children's age and how they had asked their mother and father the very same thing.

That evening, a boy and a girl raced in front of their mother and father, as they followed the path that was brightly lit by the moon. The two children could barely contain their excitement as they neared the meadow. A white light began to brighten as they neared the meadow. The children stopped. The brother and sister held each other's hand as they waited for their parents to catch up with them. Hand in hand, they continued to walk to the orchids. Suddenly, all four of them came to a halt. It did not matter how many times they had seen it before, each time was like the first time, all over again. To the little girl the moon orchids were a million white butterflies hovering above the grass as the moon orchids' stems and petals bobbed to and fro in the gentle night breeze. A tear trickled down the side of the mother's cheek. Seralyn smiled from her home high above the earth. If one were looking at the moon at that exact moment, they would have seen the moon brighten, just a little. How could the goddess not appreciate such a show of love towards her beloved children, the moon orchids? It was as it should be, but alas, it was not how it would always be.

The hearts of the humans began to change. People began to desire the beauty of the moon orchids: first, a lover wished to show the depth of his love to his beloved, so, he picked a moon orchid. The orchid cried out in its silent speech that no human could hear. Seralyn heard the last words of her child.

"Why?"

Then the orchid died, the first of many. For now, many people coveted the moon orchids' beauty. Soon, farmers wanted to use the meadows where the moon orchids grew. Whole meadows were burned so they could become fields to grow crops. Seralyn realized that her children were no longer safe where humans could find them.

So, Seralyn searched for secluded places, where humans would never venture. No more meadows filled with moon orchids, where the light of their beauty would attract the attention of humans. When Seralyn discovered a new place for her children to live, she would bring to life only a few orchids, ten or twelve at the most. It was during this time of searching when Seralyn found a spot, deep in the great forest, Yrrengh, where only enough moonlight slipped through the roof of the forest to let one moon orchid live. It was here that Lei-Shana was born. Her name meant, "the one who is alone."

Lei-Shana became the goddess's favorite child. For on all of the earth, she was the only moon orchid all by herself. Lei-Shana bore her lonely vigil well. She became friends with the animals that came to visit her. Lei-Shana's beauty and gentle spirit became known among the creatures throughout the forest Yrrengh. They called her, "The Pretty One." Thus, she lived for over a thousand years until one day she came to meet Aar-Twan, the prince who limped.

2. Aar-Twan

He was called "the prince who limps." His older brothers called him "Limpy" or "Crippy." His real name was Aar-Twan. He was named for the legendary warrior king who had united all of the tiny kingdoms in the mountains and the valleys of the rugged LeRaenian Range. Once King Aar-Twan had united all of the LeRaenian kingdoms, he led their combined armies against the fierce invaders known as "The Northern Horde", driving them back to their icy homes of the tundra and forests of the north. Thus, Aar-Twan became the first High King of LeRaen.

When Tyria, wife of Keldor, the current High King of LeRaen, was with child, she chose Aar-Twan as the child's name in the event that it was her eighth son. In the cold of Midwinter's Night, Tyria gave birth to Aar-Twan. Aar-Twan was never to see his mother, Tyria, for she died giving birth to him. Aar-Twan was born a cripple. His right foot was misshapen, bent inward from the ankle, and his right leg was slightly shriveled from his knee to his ankle. He would never be able to walk normal. When Keldor's seven older sons learned their mother had died giving birth to a cripple, they became angry.

"Father" they cried, "You cannot give a cripple the name of the greatest warrior and king in LeRaenian history!" Keldor did not answer. He sat in silence: his face frozen in pain from his beloved wife's death. Slowly, he moved his head from side to side, looking at each of his sons. Finally, he spoke, "Your mother, the queen, chose that name for your youngest brother. He shall be named Aar-Twan in honor of your mother." Braedon, the oldest son, began to speak, but was cut short by Keldor's voice, like a broadsword slicing through armor, "I Have Spoken!"

The word that Braedon had started to say hung in the air: looking for a place to hide as Braedon closed his mouth. He saw the fire in his father's eyes. It boded ill for anyone who dared to cross Keldor in such a mood. In truth, Keldor was not pleased at having a cripple for a son, much less one named Aar-Twan, but he knew that Tyria would have insisted on keeping the name they had originally chosen. That was Tyria's way, so full of love. She had to be for Keldor was not an easy man to love and he knew it. This served only to deepen Keldor's love for Tyria and now she was gone and for what? To give birth to a cripple?!

Keldor walked into his private chambers. He sat down on a high back chair and looked at the painting of Tyria hanging on the wall. Then, Keldor, High King of LeRaen, wept for the first time in his life.

3. The Youngest Prince

At first, Keldor avoided his youngest son, but as the years past and Aar-Twan began to grow in the image of his mother, Keldor could not help but see the resemblance to his beloved Tyria. After awhile, Keldor saw the unquestioning love in Aar-Twan's eyes that he had seen in Tyria. With time, the stone walls guarding his heart began to crumble: conquered by the smile of his three-year old son.

With each coming year, Aar-Twan became more like his mother: the same light auburn hair, the same smoky blue eyes, the same high cheek bones and fair skin. When he was eight years old, Aar-Twan began coming home with wild animals in his company. Keldor smiled. Tyria also had had the talent to woo wild creatures to her side. Thus, Aar-Twan, the prince who limped, lived and grew and was loved in the stout heart of his father, the High King.

The seven older brothers noticed with dismay the changed attitude of their father towards their youngest brother. Braedon ground his teeth in anger as he watched Aar-Twan go from ignored to favorite. Keldor's older sons could not understand their father's love and devotion to a cripple; so, out of their misunderstanding they avoided Aar-Twan. As Aar-Twan began to venture out to the fields and the forests outside the castle walls to visit his wild friends; his brothers could no longer completely avoid him. They watched Aar-Twan walk with his limp and amongst themselves they began to call him "Limpy" or "Crippy." They never used these names outside their brotherly circle for fear of their father's wrath. Until one day, when Aar-Twan was ten years old and Braedon could no longer hold his loathing of Aar-Twan inside himself.

Aar-Twan was returning from the forest with a wild falcon on his right arm and several small birds on his left shoulder. Braedon and the others were exercising with their broadswords by striking wooden posts. When Aar-Twan approached Braedon, Braedon stuck his sword into the ground and yelled, "Hey Limpy! Why don't you get your bird friends to carry you around? That way, you won't have to pretend you actually know how to walk!"

Aar-Twan stopped. The brothers started to laugh, then suddenly they realized what had happened; Braedon had broken the silence. Aar-Twan looked at Braedon with a puzzled expression.

"But Braedon I don't pretend to walk. I walk just as you walk."

Years of anger kept inside flew out of Braedon's mouth, like starving bats flying out of a cave.

"You do not walk like I walk. You walk like the weakling you are, with a limp: a stupid cripple, a disgrace to the Crown of LeRaen. You are not worthy of being called a LeRaenian Prince.

The other six brothers shuddered at the sound of Braedon's words. Their father would deal harshly with Braedon for his outburst, as soon as Aar-Twan told Keldor. Aar-Twan was silent. He thought about Braedon's words.

"Why do you call me a cripple?"

Braedon laughed.

"Because you have a misshapen foot and you cannot walk without limping. My brothers I believe our little brother is a dolt!"

"But Braedon, do you call a fish a cripple because it has fins and swims and cannot walk; do you call a horse a cripple because it has to run on four legs instead of two like you; do you call a bird a cripple because it has wings and flies?

"Of course not you imbecile!"

"Then why am I a cripple if I was born this way and I walk the only way I can walk?"

Braedon's mouth opened to reply, but no reply came. Aar-Twan did not wait for an answer, for to him, it was not a question. The brothers watched Aar-Twan's departure in silence. Braedon's mouth closed, but his lips curled in hate and realization; the realization that Aar-Twan would never say a word to their father about what Braedon had just said. He began to laugh.

4. The Kind Prince

Aar-Twan's seven brothers seized every opportunity to taunt him, now that they knew Aar-Twan would never tell on them to Keldor, which he never did. Neither did the teasing seem to bother Aar-Twan. This served only to convince Braedon and the others that Aar-Twan was truly a dolt, a moron. The villagers and the common folk would see the other princes verbally tormenting Aar-Twan: or at least trying their best. They would shake their heads in sadness for "the Prince who limps." That was what they called Aar-Twan amongst themselves.

The village children called Aar-Twan, "The Kind Prince" for Aar-Twan was always coming out of the forest with a new wild creature for them to see, touch, and sometimes even hold: one time it was a hawk, the next time a fox, and once he even came with a young wolf. It was this continual show of kindness towards them, the peasant children, which earned him the title of, "The Kind Prince." To the children and their parents it was not Aar-Twan who was a cripple, but his malicious brothers.

5. Bryarrgghh

One day, when Aar-Twan was fourteen years old he went into the forest to visit his best friend, Bryarrgghh the brown bear. No one else knew about Bryarrgghh. Aar-Twan never brought him to the village to see the children, for fear his brothers would want to hunt Bryarrgghh because of his great size. Aar-Twan picked his way around and over the fallen trees of the forest. It was dark among the ancient trees of the Forest Yrrengh. Hardly any light could find its way through the thick canopy of leaves. Aar-Twan had no problem finding his way, for he had exceptional night vision and knew the way very well. Finally, Aar-Twan came to the opening of a large cave, partially hidden by the foliage of a couple of small trees and some underbrush.

Aar-Twan called out, "Bryarrgghh!" He did not speak with his voice, but rather with his mind. That was Aar-Twan's gift, to be able talk to the animals with his mind. This was why the wild creatures of the forest would come to him, not as pets, but as equals who wanted to simply chat with a unique human, or even to become friends with him, as Bryarrgghh had become. A crunching of small branches and twigs announced that he was coming out of his cave. Bryarrgghh was huge. He had a reddish brown coat that would have shined if he had been in the sunlight. Each one of Bryarrgghh's four paws was four times the size of Aar-Twan's head.

Bryarrgghh spoke, "Byrring you have come. Good." With gentleness that would have surprised anyone, but Aar-Twan, Bryarrgghh's massive right paw touched Aar-Twan on his cheek.

"I have missed you Byrring." Byrring was what a bear called a cub as a form of endearment. It was Aar-Twan's name when he was with Bryarrgghh.

"Come. It is time for you to meet the 'The Pretty One.' Follow me."

Aar-Twan stood still for a second, and then began to chase after Bryarrgghh. The bear seemed to be ambling leisurely, but in fact was moving quite fast. It took Aar-Twan a little while to finally catch up to him.

"Who is 'The Pretty One'?"

"Patience Byrring. Do not act human now, but rather show why I call you son."

With that Bryarrgghh said no more. Bryarrgghh called humans, "the hasty ones", because they always seemed to be in a hurry. Aar-Twan silently followed the bear through the thick underbrush, which grew between the ancient oak and maple trees of the forest. Over huge rotting logs with mushrooms sprouting out of them, he hopped and walked. They walked over an hour. Aar-Twan's brothers would have been surprised at how nimbly he navigated around and over the various obstacles that the floor of the Forest Yrrengh presented to him. His brothers would have never kept up with Bryarrgghh's pace. They were brute force, where Aar-Twan was patience and endurance. There were many things about Aar-Twan that would have surprised Braedon and the other princes: that is because the seven older princes were not blessed with an abundance of imagination.

Bryarrgghh and Aar-Twan came to a waterfall. There they crossed a small stream that fed the waterfall and the pool below it. Aar-Twan hopped from rock to rock, while Bryarrgghh just walked through the water. Bryarrgghh began to walk down the incline that led to an open spot by the pool. There were no trees there, only rock. Over the years the force of the waterfall during the springtime floods had washed away the soil to the bare rock; no trees grew there. The absence of trees made a small opening in the forest's canopy of leaves and branches, enough of an opening for a small pillar of sunlight to come shining down on the bare rock. One did not find many such breaks in the forest's roof this deep in the Forest Yrrengh. Bryarrgghh walked to the edge of the sunlit ground and dropped his heavy haunches onto the rock. There he sat. Aar-Twan walked up to him. Bryarrgghh seemed to be staring at the sunlight pillar.

"Where is The Pretty One?"

"In the middle of the rocky opening. You must look carefully Byrring."

Aar-Twan stared, until tears began to cloud up his smoke-blue eyes. For a moment he was sure he could see the outline of something, then it disappeared.

"I can't see anything!"

"I am not surprised", said Bryarrgghh. "It is difficult for anyone to see her until they have seen her at night, when the moon is out. That is when she is at her full beauty. After that you will be able to see her during the day. We must wait. Come, you can rest by me. I will keep you warm."

"But, I can't stay until tonight! My father will become worried."

Bryarrgghh sighed.

"If you do not stay to see The Pretty One tonight Byrring, then you will never see her. No human has seen one of The Pretty One's kind, for over a thousand years. It was difficult to convince the people of the forest to even let you meet her. If you do not stay tonight, I very much doubt they would agree to give you another chance to meet her."

Aar-Twan sat down. He looked at the huge bear, who was his best friend, and asked, "Who is The Pretty One?"

"I am sorry Byrring. If you stay you will discover the answer to that question. If you do not, you will never find out."

"You are my best friend Bryarrgghh, so I trust you that to meet this Pretty One is important. I will stay."

Bryarrgghh surrounded Aar-Twan's body like a furry cocoon. All that could be seen of Aar-Twan was his face. He did not fall asleep immediately, for he was worried about his father, Keldor. Eventually, the warmth of Bryarrgghh's body snuffed out the light of Aar-Twan's thoughts, like fireflies losing their light when the morning comes.

6. The Pretty One: Lei-Shana

The moon was full. Slivers of silvery moonlight slipped through the opening in the forest's roof. The light traveled down towards the Forest Yrrengh's floor where Lei-Shana, the moon orchid, still slept. Feathers of moonlight began to tickle Lei-Shana's petals. She swayed sleepily in the gentle night breeze; her petals opened much the same way a person would yawn as they began to slowly wake up from a deep sleep. Lei-Shana looked around, not as a human looked around, but with her mind; she searched for the presence of creatures nearby. She could sense the presence of plants also, like the trees, but their minds moved in a slow manner. One tree was known to have taken ten years to answer one simple question. In other words trees did not make for good companions if you wished to have a conversation.

Lei-Shana sensed Bryarrgghh. Her heart smiled. She loved when the giant brown bear came to visit her. Bryarrgghh was by far the largest of the forest's creatures to have befriended her, but was surprisingly the most gentle of all her forest friends. Lei-Shana finally noticed Aar-Twan's head sticking out of Bryarrgghh's forelegs. She had never seen this kind of creature before; her curiosity was aroused.

"I wonder what it is?" she said to herself. "Oh, whatever it is, it is fast asleep just as Bryarrgghh is. I shall have to wait until they are awake." So, Lei-Shana opened her petals wide and drank in the moonlight streaming down from her mother's home in the sky. When she had her fill, she relaxed her petals and waited for Bryarrgghh and this other strange creature to wake up.

7. Aar-Twan Meets 'The Pretty One'

Aar-Twan's nose was cold. That was what woke him from his deep slumber in the comfort of his furry living blanket. He tried to look around, but could barely move his head. With some grunting and a lot of effort he lifted Bryarrgghh's heavy foreleg from his chest and crawled out of his furry cave. He stood up, stretched his arms and legs, and then let out a big yawn. He looked back at Bryarrgghh. His best friend was sleeping soundly. Aar-Twan turned and looked around the opening of the forest. It was then that he noticed Lei-Shana.

He froze. His eyes opened in amazement and began to water from the bright light coming from the middle of the rocky opening. He kept staring, because he was sure the bright light had something to do with The Pretty One. Slowly, a shape began to take form from the white light: first, a stem, then, an outline of petals, until finally, Aar-Twan became the first human to see a moon orchid in over a thousand years.

Lei-Shana stirred from her thoughts and noticed the strange creature staring at her. Poor thing, she thought to herself, it is afraid of me. It was normal for creatures of the forest to be afraid of her the first time they saw her. The glow of her petals actually blinded some of them for hours. I better speak to the poor creature and reassure it, she thought.

"Do not be afraid Strange One."

Aar-Twan jumped back, tripped over a log, and landed on his bottom with a look of confusion on his face. As he lay on the ground he heard laughter: laughter that sounded as if a thousand tiny crystal bells were ringing in a gentle breeze. He stood up and looked around for the source of the bell-like laughter. He found it. The laughter came from a brilliant white flower. No, not a flower, but an orchid, thought Aar-Twan. Of course that was impossible, plants don't think, much less talk was his next thought.

Lei-Shana was beside herself. The creature was funny. Never had she seen one of the forest's creatures react with so much surprise when she talked to them. Oh, I must stop laughing, Lei-Shana thought, before I scare it off for good.

The laughing stopped. Then Aar-Twan heard a voice; not a voice one hears with their ears, but with their mind. It was the type of voice that Aar-Twan used to talk to Bryarrgghh. The mind voices of the forest creatures were as unique as any voice one hears with their ears. Lei-Shan's voice was the most beautiful one that had ever filled Aar-Twan's mind.

"I am sorry poor creature. I did not mean to startle you. Please forgive my rudeness for laughing at you, but it was funny when you jumped back and tripped over the log."

Aar-Twan shook his head. He was dumbfounded, a talking flower; no, he corrected himself, a talking orchid.

"My name is Lei-Shana. What is your name?"

"Aar-Twan!", he blurted out before he realized what he was doing. "I'm talking to an orchid," he said to himself, "but that's impossible! Orchids can't talk."

"I am a moon orchid," Lei-Shana corrected him in a voice that suddenly became stern. "And why is it impossible for an orchid to talk to you? Are you so special that they don't dare speak to you?"

"No, I am not special, but I've never heard of a talking orchid before."

"Perhaps you have simply not listened!"

"Of course I've--", Aar-Twan stopped in midsentence with his mouth wide open, because actually he had never tried listening to an orchid, or any plant for that matter.

Lei-Shana had begun to think that this creature was not only rude, but not exactly the smartest animal she had ever conversed-----correction, attempted to converse with.

"I guess I've never tried talking to a flower or an orchid before, but why wouldn't they try talking to me? That's how animals talk to me."

"Well considering how rude you are it is not surprising that none of them have ever tried talking to you. Besides, most orchids are not as gregarious as animals are, being rooted to one place. It's different for me since I am a moon orchid, a daughter of Seralyn, the goddess of the moon. I am hardly common."

Aar-Twan was beginning to think this moon orchid was a bit full of herself. "The daughter of the Moon Goddess? What are you talking about? There is the Earth Mother who is a goddess and there is Jaelon, the father of the heavens, which includes the moon, naturally. Why would he need a goddess to help with just the moon?" added Aar-Twan, a bit defiantly.

"No Moon Goddess! That is simply ridiculous! If there was no Moon Goddess, then there would be no moon orchids. I have decided you are the very first creature of the forest that I do not like!"

"Well, I think you are a pompous, loudmouthed, stuffed shirt of a moon orchid!"

Lei-Shana did not know what a stuffed shirt was, but she was sure she did not like being called one. "Leave my home---you---hateful--rude --creature---whatever you are!"

"I will leave gladly, but I am not a rude creature. I am a man!'

"A man?!"

"Yes. A man, a human."

"A human!" Lei-Shana cried. Her petals clamped shut like the jaws of a trap. Lei-Shana tried to sway her body as far way from Aar-Twan as possible. Then, she screamed.

Aar-Twan's head was filled with the screams of millions of moon orchids dying in pain at the hands of their murderers, humans. He covered his ears and tried to shut out the nightmare visions that were invading him, but it did no good: the screams with their visions were already in his mind. Finally he collapsed to the ground, unconscious with blood running from his nose onto the bare rock beneath him.

8. The First Human

Bryarrgghh bounded to his feet. Each hair of his brown coat was standing on end. He tossed his head back in pain, and then he let out a roar that cut short Lei-Shana's horrific scream. Bryarrgghh shook his head, trying to rid himself of the painful images from Lei-Shana's scream. He looked around. Lei-Shana stood in the moonlight; her stem quivering so much that her petals shook. Ten feet away from her lay Aar-Twan unconscious, with blood dripping from his nose. Bryarrgghh looked at Lei-Shana.

"What have you done?!"

Lei-Shana's petals jerked back in surprise; never before had Bryarrgghh addressed her in such a tone. "What have I done?!" she cried indignantly. "What have you done, Bryarrgghh! You have brought a human into my presence; a horrible, moon orchid killing human!"

"He is not a horrible, moon orchid killing human. His name is Aar-Twan and he is a kind, loving, and gentle spirit. He is like a son to me. Aar-Twan is my best friend."

"Well, your best friend is rude!"

"Rude?" asked Bryarrgghh.

"Yes, he refused to believe that a moon orchids talk. He said he had never heard of a flower or an orchid talking before. I told him that he had probably never tried to listen to them."

Bryarrgghh snorted, "No animals are able to speak to other flowers or orchids. Perhaps they can talk, but we do not understand or hear it."

"Oh" said Lei-Shana, not so sure of herself, as she was earlier.

"What did you do when you found out he was human?"

" I did not do anything to him. I simply screamed" replied Lei-Shana.

"Yes, Pretty One, but that was no ordinary scream."

Lei-Shana hesitated before answering Bryarrgghh's question. "It was the 'Ancestral Scream." Moon orchids have a collective memory of all of the moon orchids that have died at the cruel hands of humans. So, when I screamed, it contained the pain from all of the moon orchids that have been killed by his kind", Lei-Shana said with a motion of her petals towards the still form of Aar-Twan.

A look of pain ran across Bryarrgghh's face.

"So, that was what Aar-Twan heard. No wonder my poor Byrring fainted. You must understand Lei-Shana, that only Aar-Twan has the gift of our language. The rest of humankind cannot speak to us, or has the gift of mind-speech. So, when you screamed, Aar-Twan being of such a kind and gentle spirit, died the deaths of all of the moon orchids you mourned in your scream: at least in his heart and mind. Only by fainting was he saved from actually dying by their grief; grief he had never dreamed existed. We must try and wake him."

Bryarrgghh walked over to Aar-Twan. With his right paw Bryarrgghh nudged Aar-Twan tenderly, trying to rouse him. Lei-Shana watched Bryarrgghh with her mind's eye. She saw how Bryarrgghh touched Aar-Twan, that the huge brown bear loved this human deeply. Aar-Twan moved slightly. Then suddenly he jerked his head up.

"No, nO, NOOOOO! Stop killing them!" Aar-Twan cried in torment.

Bryarrgghh wrapped his forelegs around Aar-Twan's slight body. Desperately, Aar-Twan tried to free himself. Bryarrgghh nuzzled Aar-Twan's left ear while he gently whispered in Aar-Twan's mind, "It's okay Byrring. That was a long time ago; over a thousand years have past. That is why you are the first human to see a moon orchid since that terrible time. Her mother, the Moon Goddess, hid her children from all of mankind. You were allowed to meet Lei-Shana, because only you have the gift of being able to speak with your mind. This was a gift of the Earth Mother, sister to Seralyn, the Moon Goddess.

"But, how could they kill them, Bryarrgghh? They were so beautiful" sobbed Aar-Twan.

"Aar-Twan why do your brothers hunt the wild creatures of the forest that they do not eat? Because, it gives them some kind of pleasure. The beauty of the moon orchids gave men and women pleasure: so, they began to pick them to take to their homes or give to their loved ones as presents."

"But, their cries!"

"They could not hear them Byrring. They could not hear them my son", Bryarrgghh said sadly.

Lei-Shana observed this scene with amazement. She could hardly believe this was one of the dreaded humans. He was weeping over the deaths of her brothers and sisters. Aar-Twan pulled his face away from Bryarrgghh's fur, not wet from his tears.

"Her name is Lei-Shana?" he asked in a voice that trembled.

"Yes, it is."

"I must ask her forgiveness for what humans have done to her kind."

"It is not necessary Byrring."

"Yes, it is necessary", answered Aar-Twan firmly as he looked into the large eyes of the bear towering above him. Aar-Twan walked over to Lei-Shana in his limping gait. When he reached her, he knelt down on one knee. "Please Lei-Shana forgive me for what humans have done. I realize you have every right to hate me for what I am-"

"Stop!" cried Lei-Shana. Her petals began to quiver uncontrollably. Aar-Twan looked at Bryarrgghh questioningly.

"She is crying Byrring."

"But, I didn't mean-"

"No, Aar-Twan. It is not because of you. I believe Lei-Shana is crying for what she did to you."

"She didn't mean to hurt me."

"Yes, I did", sobbed Lei-Shana. "When I discovered you were a human I wanted to make you suffer like my brothers and sisters did. So, I made you hear their cries while they died. I wanted you to die like them. I did not know that normal humans are not able to hear us, only you. It is I who should beg for your forgiveness." Lei-Shana's petals began to shake again.

"Please, Lei-Shana, do not cry. We both acted in ignorance. It wounds me even deeper to hear the most beautiful person in the world cry: especially, after I have heard her laugh. Let us be friends."

Lei-Shana's petals stopped their shaking.

"You, Aar-Twan, a human, are the most kind and gentle creature I have ever met; which is difficult to believe with knowing Bryarrgghh the Gentle. Nothing would gladden my heart more than to call you my friend, Aar-Twan."

Bryarrgghh bared his teeth in a wonderfully bearish smile.

9. Friends and Teachers

Aar-Twan and Lei-Shana became best friends. Lei-Shana also became Aar-Twan's teacher; for men had forgotten the goddesses and Aar-Twan knew nothing of them. Lei-Shana told stories of her mother, Seralyn; and of ancient times. Bryarrgghh joined Lei-Shana in teaching of the ancient lore. He explained that the Earth Mother, Maeladyth, had created the earth, its trees and plants; and all of its creatures, including humans. Everything she created, she did with the language of making, the tongue of creation. This was the language that Aar-Twan spoke with Bryarrgghh and the other people of the forest. However, humans were the only animals that could speak it out loud. It was the speaking it out loud that the power for creation was possible. Humans soon discovered the power of the language and some began to misuse the power. Therefore, Maeladyth took the knowledge of the Original Tongue away from humans and the ability to speak with their minds to others. This meant that humans could no longer communicate with other animals. In time men developed their own languages and only a few conjurers and apothecaries knew any of the creation language. They discovered these words from ancient words carved into rocks or painted on the walls of caves. They were able to use them for performing simple magic or creating potions. Aar-Twan's talent for speaking with animals, and his mother before him; was a gift from Maeladyth, the Earth Mother.

Aar-Twan learned that when humans lost their ability to speak the Original Tongue, they lost their reverence for Maeladyth and her sister, Seralyn. They began to only worship Jaelon, who they began to refer to as the One God. With the worship of Jaelon, humans lost the wisdom of how they should respect the earth and all life on the earth. They felt they were above all other creatures and began to hunt for sport, not just for food: for the pleasure of killing another life. It saddened Aar-Twan to hear this part of the story because the wild animals were his friends.

Aar-Twan never grew tired of visiting Lei-Shana: her beauty, the gentle touch of her voice on his mind; and her musical laughter that always put smile on his face and made his heart pound a little faster. Lei-Shana was amazed at the cruelty that Aar-Twan tolerated from his brothers. She begged Aar-Twan to stay in the forest with her. He would always smile at her pleas. Then Lei-Shana saw what Aar-Twan's father, Keldor saw: unquestioning love, love that even Braedon's attempts at torturing Aar-Twan could not dim. At these times, Lei-Shana felt as if her petals were about to explode with love for her dearest friend, Aar-Twan, the prince that limped.

10. Keldor's Fear

Keldor was growing old and he was afraid. Yes, Keldor, High King of LeRaen who had never lacked courage in battle was now afraid. His seven oldest sons were all great hunters, superb swordsmen, and fearless in battle, but they knew nothing of statesmanship. The oldest, Braedon only believed in survival of the fittest and had no time for discussion or talk of peace when it could be decided by the might of his arm. This was brutally apparent by Braedon's domination of his younger brothers and his mistreatment of Aar-Twan. Yes, Keldor knew about how Braedon and the other six brothers mistreated Aar-Twan. At first he was ready to banish all seven of them to their uncle Toran's manor in the country for a year. A year of cleaning up after pigs would have tempered their attitudes, he had thought, but somehow Aar-Twan had known what he was thinking. To Keldor's surprise, Aar-Twan intervened on his brothers' behalf. Keldor shook his head at the memory. Aar-Twan was just like his mother, Keldor thought to himself; even the unworthy are loved by one such as Aar-Twan.

It was apparent that none of the older sons were suited for the throne of the High King. An heir outside of Keldor's castle would have to be chosen. This would not go well with Braedon, even though Braedon was well aware that being the High King's eldest son did not mean he was assured of being chosen heir to the High King's throne. Keldor was worried about how Braedon would react to this news.

"What should I do", Keldor asked his chief advisor, Lord Chancellor Temarckan. Late into the night Keldor and Temarckan discussed how they should deal with the older princes. They came up with a plan. There was little sleep for the High King in the months that followed as the groundwork for their plan was laid. Finally, the day arrived for their plan to be carried out.

11. Keldor's Plan

All of Keldor's sons, including Aar-Twan, were gathered for the meeting. The meeting was with their father and his council of advisors. Keldor's council was made up of men from throughout LeRaen, many of them were kings of one of the small kingdoms that made up LeRaen. They were men that Keldor trusted completely and depended on their counsel to help him guide LeRaen.

Braedon was convinced that the meeting was for Keldor to officially declare Braedon as his heir to the High King's throne. What choice is there, but me, Braedon thought. Even his brothers agreed with him, but of course, they always agreed with Braedon. Keldor and his council entered the room where all of the brothers were waiting. The princes rose to their feet. Keldor walked to his chair, sat down, and motioned the rest to be seated.

"My sons, I am growing old. So, I feel, along with my advisors that before my reign as High King ends, you, my sons, should be awarded lands for your homes. My Lord Chancellor shall announce what lands each of you shall be granted."

Temarckan rose from his seat to the right of Keldor and began to speak, "I shall begin with the oldest, Braedon. In northern LeRaen there is the Kingdom of Kyria. The present king, Taeron is quite old and has no heir. King Taeron has accepted Braedon as his heir to the throne of Kyria. Congratulations Braedon, for next spring you shall be crowned the King of Kyria. King Taeron wishes to step down because of his advancing age and his failing health."

All of the older brothers began to slap Braedon on the back as they congratulated him. Braedon smiled, but inside he seethed. Only he seemed to realize what had just happened: he, Braedon, the oldest son of the High King of LeRaen was not to be the heir to his father's throne.

12. The Hunt

Winter came. Ice coated the stones of the High King's castle. Fires burned bright, but nothing could warm the cold of Braedon's heart. Outwardly, he acted excited about becoming the King of Kyria; inwardly, bitter thoughts of a pebble-sized kingdom rather than his father's throne, lived in his mind like worms in a rotten apple.

Braedon's bitterness had only one outlet, taunting Aar-Twan. Aar-Twan had also been granted land: a country manor with land bordering the forest that Aar-Twan loved so dearly. Keldor knew in a small estate the people would learn to love and respect a kind and gentle lord such as Aar-Twan. Braedon however, could not believe that even Aar-Twan had been given land. How could they grant land to a weakling, a cripple, thought Braedon. It did not matter that the lands were small and worth little. Braedon began to think of new ways to torment his youngest brother, until one day he thought of the perfect scheme; the most delightful trick he had ever stumbled on, a hunt; a bear-baiting hunt.

Bear baiting was done in the winter. Several hunters would go into the forest, find a bear cave, and then they would proceed to wake the bear with whatever means was necessary. When the bear woke and came out of its cave it would be in a foul mood from being roused from its winter sleep. The bear would come out and be met by the hunters with their spears, and the hunters would proceed to try and kill the bear. Bear baiting was extremely dangerous and many times more than one hunter was injured, or even killed. However, the bear hardly ever escaped. It was a cruel sport, which is why Braedon enjoyed it so much. It was his plan to go on a bear-baiting hunt with all of his brothers, including Aar-Twan. He told Keldor that he and his brothers wanted to simply hunt for rabbits and deer. Braedon explained to Keldor that it would be a brotherly last hurrah, before they all left for their separate domains in the spring. Keldor thought it was a great idea. He felt good about Braedon wanting to include Aar-Twan. Although Aar-Twan did not care for hunting, he would have to get used to it eventually was Keldor's thinking. Hunting was an important source of food at Aar-Twan's new country estate. He might as well start becoming accustomed to the idea now, mused Keldor.

Aar-Twan was told nothing about their winter excursion being a hunt. On the day of trip, Braedon wasted no time; he took his brothers straight to a cave deep in the Forest Yrrengh that he had recently found while following Aar-Twan, curious as to what Aar-Twan did by himself in the forest. It was Bryarrgghh's home. "Grandon" barked Braedon, "Pass out the spears!"

Aar-Twan of course knew it was Bryarrgghh's cave immediately. He always missed Bryarrgghh during the winter months, when the huge bear would hibernate. It made Aar-Twan feel good, just to see the home of his friend. Aar-Twan noticed Grandon fetching spears from the packhorse.

"What do we need spears for?" he asked.

"For hunting of course, little brother" Braedon said with a sneer.

"But you never mentioned hunting."

"Did you think we were taking a winter excursion for the beautiful scenery?"

The brothers laughed at Braedon's remark. Braedon took a spear and shoved it into Aar-Twan's hand.

"What are we going to hunt?" asked Aar-Twan, as he felt the cold shaft of the spear in his hand, a hand that had never held a spear before. Braedon smiled, then he pointed to Bryarrgghh's cave. A look of horror came over Aar-Twan's face.

"But you can't! Bryarrgghh is my friend. He's sleeping!"

"Did you say the bear is your friend?" Braedon asked with a laugh. "Come now little brother are your daft? You may be able to call a few harmless animals to you, but a bear? That's impossible!"

"Please Braedon" Aar-Twan pleaded. Tears began to cloud his eyes.

"Shut Up! You will do exactly as I say! Telar-Din! Kamerill! Light the torches! We need to start a fire. Come on! Move!"

The brothers threw wood into a pile for a bonfire. Soon, they had a large fire burning. They took some of burning brands and threw them into the cave's opening. Then, they started to throw rocks into the cave in hopes of striking the bear to help wake it up. When the brothers heard some grunting coming from the cave, they formed a half circle around the entrance. Aar-Twan stood silent, still holding the spear that Braedon had forced into his hand. It had become like a cancer growing from his hand that he could not get rid of. Suddenly, the form of Bryarrgghh appeared at the cave's entrance.

The brothers, even Braedon, all gasped: never had they seen such a gigantic bear. Bryarrgghh stood on his hind legs. His eyes blinked from the brightness and smoke of the bonfire. Bryarrgghh was tired, hungry, and upset at having his midwinter's sleep disturbed. He looked around and saw the men with spears. Bryarrgghh knew what the spears meant. Then, he saw Aar-Twan standing in the middle of the half circle with a spear in his hand.

"No, not you Byrring."

Aar-Twan's mind was frozen. He did not know what to say or do.

"How could the one I call my son betray me!" Bryarrgghh let out a tremendous roar of pain. Blind with the fury of betrayal, he rushed Aar-Twan. With one swat, he sent Aar-Twan flying into the snow bank. Aar-Twan began to bleed from where Bryarrgghh's claws had cut into his side. Bryarrgghh raced to where Aar-Twan landed and then raised his paw to deliver a killing blow to Aar-Twan. Aar-Twan's eyes opened. He looked into Bryarrgghh's large brown eyes and linked minds with the great bear. Immediately Bryarrgghh realized that Aar-Twan had not betrayed him, but had been tricked by his brothers.

The other seven brothers were paralyzed with astonishment. Never had they seen such a huge bear. Never, had they seen a bear attack with such speed and ferocity. The huge brown bear rushed to where its blow had sent Aar-Twan flying, then raised its paw for the death blow, Suddenly, it stopped, dropped down to all fours beside Aar-Twan and the two seemed to lock eyes. The brothers were held in a trance watching this strange sight. Then Braedon broke out of his stupor, pulled back his spear, and heaved it with all his might at the bear. The bear roared it pain as the spear entered his side. Bryarrgghh's roar woke the other brothers from their trance and stirred them into action. They proceeded to throw their spears into Bryarrgghh. Bryarrgghh roared in pain and then fell down with his blood beginning to color the snow bright red.

"No" shouted Aar-Twan. Ignoring the pain from his wound from the claws of Bryarrgghh, he rose to his feet and hobbled over to the bear. Tears streamed down his cheeks. "Forgive me Bryarrgghh, I didn't know."

"Forgive me, my son, for I should have known" Those were the last words of Bryarrgghh the brown bear, one of the best friends of Aar-Twan the prince who limped. Aar-Twan clutched the fur of Bryarrgghh, as he sobbed uncontrollably. He was unaware of his brothers as they approached him. Braedon grabbed Aar-Twan by the scruff of his neck and pulled him away from the dead bear.

"Come on crybaby, we men have a bear to skin."

"No!" screamed Aar-Twan. "You hateful creature. You murdered my best friend." Aar-Twan grabbed his fallen spear and stabbed Braedon in his thigh. Braedon's eyes opened wide with shock, then quickly clouded with rage.

"You insolent cripple, I will kill you for that!" Braedon reached for his sword but Aar-Twan ran off into the forest he knew so well, leaving only a trail of blood.

13. Aar-Twan's Final Destination

Aar-Twan stumbled, fell to his knees, then slowly picked himself up, and then continued his journey. Through knee high drifts of snow, Aar-Twan trudged with the wind biting at his cheeks and branches snapping at his face, as he tried to push them out of his way. Aar-Twan kept walking. He no longer felt pain, cold, or the dampness that had invaded the soles of his boots. His shirt was now red and stiff from his blood that had soaked the cloth and then was frozen solid by the icy breath of the winter night. A lifeline made of love and friendship pulled Aar-Twan's heart and feet to his destination, Lei-Shana's home. He came to the frozen stream. The snow made a crunching sound as Aar-Twan walked up the bank to where the snow could not gain a strong foothold on the slippery rock where Lei-Shana's stem was anchored.

"Aar-Twan!" Lei-Shana cried, as she sensed his presence and his weakened state.

Aar-Twan did not answer. He fell to his knees, flopped face down, with his bloodless lips kissing the thin layer of snow on the rock. His wound began to bleed. The snow around Lei-Shana began to turn red.

"Aar-Twan! Aar-Twan! What is wrong?"

Aar-Twan groaned, rolled to his side, and opened his eyes. He looked at the beautiful petals of his friend, Lei-Shana.

"What is the matter Aar-Twan?" Lei-Shana asked as her petals began to tremble with worry.

"I am dying, Lei-Shana."

"Dying!" cried Lei-Shana. "You can't be dying. Aar-Twan, where is Bryarrgghh? We need Bryarrgghh! He will know what to do."

"Bryarrgghh is dead. My brothers murdered him."

"But why?" Lei-Shana asked. Her petals started quivering as she tried to keep from crying.

Aar-Twan began to speak, but stopped, as a spasm shook his entire body.

"AAR-TWAN!"

The spasm ended. Aar-Twan's eyes could barely focus on the white form of Lei-Shana. His lips barely moved as he spoke with both his voice and mind.

"At least I am dying with you, my best friend."

"Aar-Twan why do you have to die?!"

"Lei-Shana, I love you" he whispered.

Lei-Shana felt Aar-Twan's mind slipping away. She knew he was about to die. She opened her petals wide and screamed: the scream of a million moon orchids dying at once.

14. The Earth Mother and the Moon Goddess

Lei-Shana's cry could be heard from the center of the moon to the core of the earth. Maeladyth, the Earth Mother, was busy in her home deep in the earth, preparing for the coming spring. She heard Lei-Shana's scream; never, had Maeladyth heard such pain. She searched for the source of the cry with her mind's eye. She found Lei-Shana sobbing and beside her was Aar-Twan. Maeladyth recognized Aar-Twan immediately, for it she who had given him the gift of the First Tongue and the ability to speak with his mind.

She knew Aar-Twan was dead. This is terrible she thought. How could I have been so preoccupied with spring to have missed this; then she noticed his blood soaking the snow covering the rock around Lei-Shana's stem.

"Oh No" she said to herself, "She will die if his blood reaches her petals"; for human blood was poisonous to moon orchids. "Seralyn will be furious", she groaned. She knew that Lei-Shana was her sister's favorite child among the moon orchids. There was already bad blood between Maeladyth and her sister; ever since the first foolish human picked a moon orchid to give to his lover. Since, humans were Maeladyth's creation, Seralyn held her responsible for what they did to the moon orchids. I must leave at once. A bubble formed out of the molten rock and swooshed her towards the surface and Lei-Shana's home in the Forest Yrrengh.

In the center of the moon, Seralyn knew instantly that it was Lei-Shana who had screamed.

"Lei-Shana!"

Without a pause, she called her winged steed, Aradorn. A cloud of white mist appeared in front of her; then it changed into a large white stallion with wings. She pounced onto Aradorn's back.

"Take me to Lei-Shana! She is in grave danger!"

With a toss of his powerful head that sent waves rippling though his mane and an angry snort of his nostrils, Aradorn leaped earthward.

15. World Crossed Lovers

Aar-Twan lay motionless. He was dead and Lei-Shana knew it and now it was to late to tell him that she was in love with him. Watching him die by her side had led Lei-Shana to that realization. She watched Aar-Twan's blood seep into her stem. She understood what that meant, as soon as the blood reached her petals, she would die. She did not care; without Aar-Twan, Lei-Shana had no desire to go on living.

"I love you Aar-Twan," sobbed the beautiful moon orchid named, 'The One Who Is Alone' in a language she had once shared with Aar-Twan, 'The Prince that Limped.'

16. Two Sisters

The ground opened like the mouth of a great Dragon as Maeladyth stepped out of her travel-bubble. The onyx hooves of Aradorn announced the arrival of Seralyn. When his hooves struck the rocks of Lei-Shana's home, sparks went flying while steam shot out from Aradorn's nostrils. His chest heaved from flying so fast from the moon as Seralyn flew from his back to her daughter's side.

"Oh, my poor child!"

Lei-Shana's stem was completely red, while her petals were streaked with the color of blood. The Moon Goddess moaned in despair; she knew it was too late to save her favorite daughter.

"I can save her", said Maeladyth.

"How can you save her, when the foul blood of your murdering children has already reached her innocent petals?"

"You did not have to bear your children in my domain, Seralyn, but I did not come to fight with you sister. So, for the good of Lei-Shana and Aar-Twan, let us set aside our differences. I can save her, but not as a moon orchid. She will become a woman with her heart made from the moon orchid. She will remain part moon orchid and will retain all of her past moon orchid memories. Thus, she will still be your daughter."

"I will not consent to my daughter becoming a human: an eagle, a wolf, or even a rabbit, but never a human!"

"Then you do not really love your daughter."

"Maeladyth, you old hag! How dare you say such a thing!"

"I dare, because if you truly love Lei-Shana you would not separate her from her true love, Aar-Twan."

"Lei-Shana in love with this bony man? Impossible!"

"Of all my brothers and sisters, you, Seralyn are the most vain! Now your vanity extends to how you think of your own children. Look into Lei-Shana's mind before it is too late. Then tell me it is impossible!"

Seralyn was silent for a brief moment. She looked away from Maeladyth.

"So, it is true, but your Aar-Twan is dead. It would be more cruel for me to let you change her into a woman then to let her die as a moon orchid."

Aar-Twan can live again if you replace the blood that he has lost with moonlight."

"But that would make him immortal!"

"Not immortal. He would live a very long time as would Lei-Shana."

"I will do it."

"Then, you must act quickly, before Aar-Twan's spirit has wandered too far from his body."

The goddess of the moon pointed her right index finger at Aar-Twan. A shaft of moonlight shot out into Aar-Twan's wounds; the white light began to mix with his cold blood. A glowing whiteness spread throughout his body. The claw marks disappeared and his chest began to rise up and down. Aar-Twan was once again alive, and sleeping soundly.

"Good, his spirit has returned. You were in time." chimed Maeladyth.

"Now it is your turn sister. Do what you must, but save my daughter" replied Seralyn.

Maeladyth bent down and plucked Lei-Shana from her stony home. The moon orchid felt nothing, so close to death she was. Maeladyth placed her gently on the snow. Then she began making a woman's body from the snow. She gave Lei-Shana bright auburn hair made from the leaves of autumn, red lips she gave her from the blood of Aar-Twan, her silver-blue eyes came from his frozen tears, and finally she took the moon orchid's body to make a heart that she placed inside the woman's body. The pale beautiful woman began to breathe. After awhile she stirred; her eyes fluttered and then opened. The woman saw Seralyn standing over her with a look of concern.

"Mother, you've come. I thought I was dead", Lei-Shana said as she sat up. She realized something was wrong. She looked at horror at her human hands, her arms, her legs, and her entire human body.

"Where are my petals? What has happened?"

"You are a human, my child" Seralyn whispered.

"But I don't want to be a human!"

"It was the only way we could save you. The human blood had reached your petals before I could arrive. Your moon orchid body was used to make your human heart, so you are still my daughter, my favorite daughter. Lei-Shana the moon orchid is now a human, but no longer are you Lei-Shana."

"What do you mean I am no longer Lei-Shana?"

"She means you are no longer alone. Now you are free to love Aar-Twan as your human lover", replied Maeladyth.

"But, Aar-Twan is dead", Lei-Shana whispered as her first human tear trickled down her cheek.

"He was dead. Now, he is alive. It is my gift to you, my beloved daughter", said Seralyn. "I replaced the blood he lost with moonlight. Now he is a child of both the earth and moon, just as you are."

"Where is he?"

Maeladyth smiled. "He is over there, child. He still sleeps, for he was dead, where you were only near death. He will sleep for a time, yet. Love him well Lei-Shana, for I, Maeladyth the earth mother have few human children that I am as proud of as Aar-Twan. Now, I think your mother and I should leave you alone with your love. Come Seralyn. I would like to show you my home. I have made a few changes in the last thousand years."

Then Lei-Shana found herself alone as she watched Aar-Twan breathing in and out as she sat patiently by his side for him to wake.

17. The Broken Land

When Braedon and his brothers returned from the forest with news of Aar-Twan's death, it was too much for Keldor. When he lost the love of his life, Tyria the queen, it had almost overcome the High King's stout heart. Now, losing Aar-Twan and the love that his youngest son had given to him, was more than Keldor could bear. His heart was truly broken. Keldor died in his sleep that same night.

With the death of Keldor and no heir having been named, Braedon seized the opportunity to declare himself High King. Lord Chancellor Temarckan challenged Braedon's claim, because he knew his friend, Keldor would have wanted Braedon stopped. This resulted in a civil war that was to last many years and caused LeRaen to be splintered into many tiny kingdoms continually feuding with each other.

All of this took place while the two goddesses were busy saving Aar-Twan and Lei-Shana, for time does not proceed at the same pace for gods and goddesses. A few minutes for them, were years for the people of LeRaen.

18. Lei-Shana and Aar-Twan

Lei-Shana sat by the still form of Aar-Twan. She did not know what to do, so she simply sat, and continued to watch the rise and fall of his chest. Aar-Twan let out a sigh. Lei-Shana knelt down by him and gently touched her lips to his cheek. Then, for the first time in her life, she kissed her love on his lips.

Aar-Twan's eyes began to flutter. He blinked. He saw a strange woman with the most beautiful pale skin he had ever seen looking down at him. Something about her was familiar, but he was sure he had never met her before.

"How are you feeling my love?" the woman asked in a voice like crystal teardrops.

Aar-Twan's eyes opened wide in surprise. He tried to stand up. He slipped with a thunk in a shallow snow bank. Then he heard laughter; laughter that sounded as if a thousand tiny bells were ringing. He knew that laugh. It was Lei-Shana's laugh, but this time he was hearing it with his ears, not his mind.

"Lei-Shana?"

"Yes, Strange One. Did I frighten you?"

"But—you're human!"

"Yes, I am now a human. I am a woman who loves a man. A man named Aar-Twan."

Aar-Twan was still bewildered by just being alive, but to look in the eyes of Lei-Shana the woman----all he could so was shake his head.

"It is a long story, which I shall tell you, but first I wish to touch you, hold you in my arms, and kiss my one and only true love; even when I was a moon orchid."

Lei-Shana extended her hand to Aar-Twan, helping him to stand up. He was about to ask another question when he looked into her eyes. The question vanished. Instead, Aar-Twan found himself holding Lei-Shana in his arms while they kissed, and kissed, and kissed.

19. Lei-Shana the Human

Aar-Twan thought he would be happy the rest of his life, if all he did was wander through the forest while holding Le-Shana's hand. Lei-Shana told Aar-Twan the story of how she became human and how her mother brought him back to life. Incredible as that story was, it paled in comparison to the love he saw in Lei-Shana's eyes.

Lei-Shana was still getting used to her human body. She was like a newborn colt, learning how to run and jump, or simply lying on the ground while staring at the different shapes of the clouds in the sky. Watching her frolic made Aar-Twan smile and laugh. He watched as she got on her hands and knees to smell a flower that had sprouted where she had once been a moon orchid. Suddenly, Aar-Twan realized something was not quite right.

"Lei-Shana, how long has it been since we first kissed?"

"Why only a couple of weeks silly!"

"Then why is it spring?" asked Aar-Twan. "It was winter when I came to you and I was dying." I've been so lost in love that I did not even notice the change in season, thought Aar-Twan.

Lei-Shana was quiet for a moment before she tried to answer Aar-Twan's question.

"Time is not the same for the gods and goddesses. A year for us might be nothing more than a minute to them. I am not sure, but when Maeladyth and my mother, Seralyn were busy saving us, we might have been temporarily caught up in their time, so that years past for the world when only minutes passed for you and me. That is the only explanation I can come up with my love."

A look of concern came over Aar-Twan's face.

"I need to know how much time has passed. My father probably thinks I am dead. I need to go back to his castle and tell him I am okay. I will only leave for a little while. You do not need to come."

"No! I will not let you leave me again. I am no longer a moon orchid rooted to one place; I am a woman and will remain by your side."

Lei-Shana wrapped her arms around Aar-Twan's shoulders and held him tight, very tight.

20. The Return

Aar-Twan and Lei-Shan left the next morning. As they walked through the forest, they did not say a word. Somehow, they knew there would never be another two weeks in their life like the last two weeks. When the two of them came to the edge of the forest, Maeladyth was waiting there with two pure white horses by her side.

Lei-Shana walked up to the Earth Mother and put her arms around the goddess in an embrace: a silent thank you for what Maeladyth had done for her. Aar-Twan stood still. He had already guessed who the strange woman was. This did not set him at ease. It was not an everyday occurrence that one met the creator of their world. Maeladyth looked at Aar-Twan as Lei-Shana stepped back from her. A smile played on her lips at seeing Aar-Twan's discomfort.

"Do not be afraid my son. Come closer, so I may see you better", said Maeladyth in a voice, soft and gentle, but more commanding than Aar-Twan's father when he was angered.

Aar-Twan approached the Earth Mother. He stopped when he came face to face with her. Maeladyth looked at Aar-Twan with smiling eyes.

"When I look into your heart Aar-Twan I see a painful question. That is the reason I have come: to answer that question and more. As you have guessed, it is not the same time as when you came to Lei-Shana dying. Twenty years have passed since then."

"But how", interrupted Aar-Twan.

"Time for myself and Seralyn is not the same as it is for humans and the rest of the world. Twenty years for a human is but a brief moment for me. When my sister and I were saving you and Lei-Shana, you entered into our time: so, twenty years became minutes to you also. One does not create or recreate hastily, Aar-Twan. It is a price you must pay for being alive again. Now, I must warn you; much as changed in LeRaen since you were reawakened. When your brothers returned, they informed your father, that you a bear killed you. The pain was too much for your father and he died in his sleep that very same night. With no heir chosen for the High King's throne, Braedon declared himself the High King. Lord Temarckan refused to acknowledge Braedon's claim to the throne and LeRaen was thrown into a civil war that lasted over ten years. Neither side won. LeRaen was split into many small kingdoms that are constantly bickering and fighting. It is worse than before Aar-Twan the First united them. Much of the land has been laid to waste and there are mercenaries from the war that now make their living by robbing travelers and raiding villages. The land is in need of a ruler who is kind and loving. It is time for The Kind Prince to return to his people."

"But they are not my people."

"Aar-Twan only you of all your father's sons, captured the hearts of the LeRaenian people. Not even your father was as deeply loved as you were. Keldor inspired respect, fear, and trust, but love was not something that came to Keldor easily. The land is in need of love so it can heal. Take these horses as your mounts. They have the blood of the unicorn in them. You will need no saddles or bridles to ride them. They will carry you as fast as the wind. Care for them well. Now go!"

The two horses knelt down on their forelegs so that Aar-Twan and Lei-Shana could mount them more easily, because of their great size. Then before they could even take another breath, the two horses were galloping like the wind. Aar-Twan glanced back in Maeladyth's direction, but she was already out of sight. He turned and looked at Lei-Shana. She smiled. He smiled back, and then turned to look ahead as they both road towards their future.

21. Epilogue

When the moon is full, children beg their mother and father to take them for a moonlit walk to the place where they could see the east wall of the High King's castle. There they would wait at the edge of the forest, hoping to catch a glimpse of the High King and is beautiful High Queen, as they came out to their balcony. There the couple would stand with their arms around each other's waists, while they seemed to soak up the moonlight. The light from the moonlight would make their skin glow and the Queen's hair appear on fire. If the children were really lucky, they would see the High King Aar-Twan and the High Queen Lei-Shana turn, look into each other's eyes, embrace, and finally, kiss.